THE SILENT INVADER

BOOK 1 IN THE 'GLIDERS OVER NORMANDY'
SERIES

THOMAS WOOD

This book is dedicated to all the men who took part in Operation Deadstick, in what became known as the raid on Pegasus Bridge, with a particular dedication to those who lost their lives that night and in the following days and months of the Second World War.

Other books in the 'Gliders over Normandy' series:

- 'The Silent Invader' (2017)
- 'All Men are Casualties' (2018)
- 'As if they were my own' (2018)

1

As we'd lurched off the ground, bumping around and hitting every groove in the strip as was possible, my stomach felt as if it was going to break through the back of my seat. It was a sensational feeling, and one that I could never quite get used to, especially when I became convinced that the force of the tow rope tightening, as the tug yanked us forward, would rip the front of the glider clean off.

The constant low rumble of engines and the enraging creaking from the joins in the framework, that had frequented my ears for hours, began to bore into my mind and echoed in my eardrums. I had become so used to the sound, from hours of training flights and landings, that it had almost given me a solace, provided me with an element of consistency, as I flew into a world that would be anything but.

The soft detachment of the tow rope was a blessed relief as the low drone of engines slowly faded off into the darkness, our engines, on their way home. I felt almost sorry for them, as they departed, they still had to fly onwards some more, bomb a target as a diversion, and then negotiate their way back over the plethora of coastal defences that we had only just put behind us.

My co-pilot took his hand off the release lever and looked over to me. He'd yanked it backwards so vigorously that I half expected it to come off in his hand, leaving us in a never-ending circle of being towed around the skies. He gave me a semi-smile, the kind that two school boys give each other, when they realise they have just got away with the biggest crime of the century.

I noticed his hand was quivering slightly, but his eyes were fired with determination and excitement. I gave him a flick of a smile. Giving him a glimmer of a smile in return, I knew that the quiver that was slowly taking hold of his hand wouldn't have been out of fear, but probably due to the sheer amount of adrenaline that was surging through his body. I knew that because I was feeling exactly the same. As I continued to look at him, for half a second too long, my thoughts were interrupted by a voice.

"Good luck chaps," had sparked a crackled voice over the radio, before our communication line too, was released. The voice was confident, reassuring almost, and it filled me with a fantastic amount of gratefulness to the boys who had towed us into such a hostile environment. I was in awe of them, they had completed so many ops over enemy held territory, some of them already on their second tour, completely voluntarily. I only hoped that my bravery would extend to somewhere close to the amount they displayed.

The crackled voice had carried a message that did not need an acknowledgement and, even if it did, my full attention was now on my aircraft and my cargo, not the aircraft that was pulling away from us at a couple of hundred miles an hour.

All that I could hear now was the creaking as men shuffled around in their kit, itching to get out of the flying coffin they were in. No one seemed to dare to speak, as if their voices would put us all at risk and threaten the entire operation. As soon as the shuffling had started, it stopped almost immediately, and I felt the expectation on my shoulders grow as they all held their breath and said a prayer for me.

We lost altitude rapidly as we were released, but as I forced the plane into a snaking motion of left banking and right, we began to descend at a much more graceful pace. I was trying to manipulate one of the biggest and most well-known forces known to man, gravity. I needed to maintain a decent enough speed, to try and keep the amount of thrust we needed to stay airborne for as long as possible, but it was difficult, especially when I had such a heavy load on board.

The controls began squeaking as I used my strength to guide the men down to our landing site. I grunted with exertion as my co-pilot fought with the rudder to control our movements.

His head pivoted like an owl on drugs as he scanned the countryside below for some reference points. We would try our best to stay in the air until his eyes, trained as good as a hawk's, spotted something that told us where we were. His head movements and his eyes began to work together, his eye balls rolling around in their sockets, trying to broaden the horizons of his vision, but it seemed like he was struggling to make out anything that he recognised.

Momentarily, I helped him. The landscape below was in total darkness, as if an inky blanket had been pulled over the top, hiding everything useful from our gaze. I had half expected to see a big arrow, pointing us to our drop zone, as I had become so accustomed at staring at the reconnaissance photos that had done just that for us during training. The other side of my brain anticipated seeing gunfire making its way up to us, or to see firefights raging below as the various groups of pathfinders became the first men of the invasion force to be engaged. But I saw nothing, just a barren landscape of fields, obscured by the rolling, wispy clouds.

We were looking for a river. The moon glinted down on the land below, but I could see no distinguishing features that I recognised.

My hands gripped the central control a lot tighter as I turned my gaze from the front, a nervous disposition that I had never been quite able to shift. The controls felt warm and were layered with a thick coating of sweat from my hands. I had ditched my gloves just before we were released.

It wasn't protocol or routine, just another of my dispositions, we all had them. I felt closer to the aircraft when I felt skin on the controls, I became an integral part in the construction of the craft.

I once voiced my preference to be able to fly naked if I had been allowed to, an opinion that my co-pilot, very aggressively, did not share.

I turned my eyes to the front again and gazed out of the paper-thin wind shield we had in front of us. A reminder of how basic our cockpit truly was. We couldn't afford to be flying with no engines and heavy electrical equipment. We had the basics.

A few instruments; altimeter, airspeed indicator, that sort of thing and most important of all, the brake lever. That was it. There was no throttle, no sort of emergency power that we could utilise if we found ourselves heading towards a ditch or a lake, there was absolutely nothing that we would be able to use if we found ourselves in trouble. We had no option of bailing out, no option of returning to base, we were now fully committed to this invasion.

I thought how much like a paper aeroplane we must have looked like, with our oversized wings and how the glider had been constructed out of one type of flimsy, cheap material. But we were even more like a paper plane in the way we majestically fell to the ground, completely at the mercy of the gentle breeze around us, with little say as to where we landed and when.

I only hoped that we didn't crumple on the ground like a piece of flimsy paper.

I felt like I'd become an expert in landing the silent craft but that was in daylight, there was no one shooting at us and, it was on flat terrain. I hated being in so much control, the way that the boys in the back were having to put their faith in me completely and yet, no matter how many training missions that we had completed, there was still such a large amount of uncertainty looming over me, an uncertainty over which I had little control.

I was amazed at how we'd made it through a barrage of searchlights as we'd passed over the French coast. They flickered teasingly across the belly of our aircraft then passed silently over the underside of the Halifax in front. I had been blinded for a moment as one stream had caught on the rear gunner's windshield, sending a shrieking burst of light directly into my unprotected eyes. They continued to taunt us, lighting up the cockpit every now and then, before leaving us, as if they hadn't quite seen us.

We had no option but to fly on, unperturbed by the passing lights.

The ack ack guns however, jostled us about like a bully in the school yard, throwing the occupants of our craft around like ragdolls. It wasn't so much the feeling of the anti-aircraft guns that was making me feel nervous, but the noise that resounded each time a volley was fired towards us, like the drumbeat as it grew progressively quicker the closer it came to execution time.

I forced that image from my mind as my neck clicked several times as it was pushed from side to side, backwards and forwards as somehow the guns missed their targets.

The singing of the men had gradually grown fainter as the repetitive booming of the anti-aircraft guns had grown dimmer. It was almost as if, the closer we had got to our target, the more their confidence had waned. I wondered for a moment if there had been any additional takers on the hip flask that had been passed around shortly after take-off, especially after our dalliance with the searchlights.

Now, we were just left, silently floating through the night sky, like Death seeking out his next victim, ready to wreak havoc on the world below.

I felt powerful up in the sky, like a god about to release punishment and destruction on his subjects with no mercy. I began to feel a rage burn up inside me, placing the fear in my mind towards the back. It spurred me on and I felt myself straining my eyes even more as the anger morphed into a brilliant determination, that I had never experienced before. I suddenly found myself locked in a silent competition with my co-pilot, I desperately wanted to be the one to spot our landing site first, even though it made no real difference, just as long as we found it.

The whoosh of the wind intensified as we lowered, it almost became unbearable as we excitably drifted. The rustling of the wind as it swooped over our wings, began to transform into what felt more like a scream, a primitive howl. I hoped earnestly that we were the only ones being subjected to this crescendo, and that no one below us would even hear a vague whisper of it.

Suddenly, as I continued my pointless competition, the inky blanket was lifted, as we descended below the clouds.

We were no longer blind. We could see.

2

From a young age, I'd always toyed with the idea of becoming a soldier, but truthfully, I'd never had the guts to do so. I loved the image of running around with a gun in my hands, taking the life of an enemy who'd murdered and raped, a hero ridding the world of the scum of the earth. The idea of helping to right the world of its wrongs and get attention and recognition in the form of medals and parades appealed to me. I was fit enough, there was no doubt about it, and I'd always had an adventurous streak that meant I spent large amounts of my time outside, days at a time, on occasion.

I loved it all, the adventure, the excitement, the admiration, but I hadn't liked the idea of being shot at, or watching my friends die helplessly in battle.

I'd been in the local church choir; my mother had made me join in the hope I would gain a respect for the church instead of throwing hymn books around and passing wind in services. I had hated it, leading to endless teasing from the other local lads who were dragged along on a Sunday to hear our renditions of certain hymns and endless performances around Christmas time. If anything, my time in the choir had had the opposite effect upon me that my mother had desired, the numerous times I plodded into St Michael's meant that each time I lost a little bit more of the awe and admiration I had for the church. There was just one event that had changed my perception of it, and it made me grateful for my position in the stalls of the choir.

Every year, from the year I'd first joined the choir, I'd been struck with pride, but also humbleness at the men who shuffled in on the day of remembrance. Each one was able to hold themselves well, but, on that one day of the year I watched as their shoulders slouched forwards slightly, as each of them kept their eyes fixed on the ground as if they were looking for a misplaced shilling.

They were people I'd grown up around, teachers, postmen and even clergymen. I knew them all by name, I could tell you where they lived and who they were married to.

I bid them a good day every time I saw them about, and they returned it with a broad smile. It was only that one day a year though, that I viewed them as soldiers. As heroes.

Their medals would always clink together and reverberate off the stone walls of the church, as they tried in vain to sit down silently by separating their medals with their fingers. I'd never quite understood their modesty. From my premium seat in the stalls, I could marvel at their medals and the wide variety of colours of their ribbons that adorned their chests, each one depicting a heroic or chivalrous act to my young imagination.

My father's own medals never left the house, I only knew that they even existed because I was playing a rather immature game of hide and seek with my sister.

I found a stash containing letters, photographs and a Bible, stuffed nonchalantly into the smallest box possible. I couldn't imagine why a man, let alone a war hero, would treat such items in this way. I couldn't get my head around the fact that this man was not shouting about his exploits, not telling as many people as possible about what he had done, not even on Remembrance Day. I charged down the stairs, clutching the small trinket box that enclosed my new-found artefacts, before I set about exploring each one in detail on the kitchen table.

"Where on earth did you find that?!" My mother had shrieked upon entering the room.

"Charlie, get that box out of here now, and put it back where you got it from, before your Dad gets back!"

That was all that was ever said in my house about that after that incident, my Dad evidently moving the box to a new location shortly after.

He'd always walked with a limp for as long as I could remember, but I'd never known why, just walking round the park would render him breathless. He relied on his stick everywhere he went, never standing up straight but always leaning on it.

It had a tough job in keeping such a big man like my dad upright. We knew never to ask about it. After the incident with the trinket box, I knew that that was a chapter of my Dad's life that he never wanted to return to, never wanting to reflect on it even. So, the lid of the trinket box, as well as the lid that stored the stories of how my Dad possessed an odd walking pattern, remained firmly on, never seeing the light of day in our household.

I never listened to those church services, I stared intently at their chests and marvelled at what each piece of highly polished metal represented.

I dreamed up stories of their heroics, rescuing friends in a hail of bullets and saving children from certain destruction. I wondered how many more medals would have been given out if half of the men who had died had in fact, survived the Great War. My young, immature, mind, found it difficult to envisage these middle-aged, balding and weary looking men, gallantly fighting and capable of heroics. I could not imagine what they had looked like in their youth, when they had been teenagers rather than forty-year-old men. I could not imagine that what they had seen would have given me nightmares for weeks, if not months, never mind what it did to their own dreams.

As I grew older, I began to understand, to appreciate what they had done and seen. So much so that even though I wanted to join up, I would never be able to truly compare myself to those men. I never thought I'd get the opportunity to display what little courage and bravery I had; I had worked as a butcher's apprentice until a few years ago, and even the sight of a small amount of pig's blood had been enough to send me into a never-ending cycle of nausea and light headedness.

Everyone else was signing up, so why shouldn't I? That was my reasoning. I had more courage in a pack of friends, boys on their own are never confident in anything.

My mother didn't have the exact same outlook, she had paced around the kitchen screaming.

"Your Dad! Look what it did to him! He's never been the same and now you're going!"

There was no talking her down, she'd made up her mind at the outbreak of war that I wasn't to go, in her mind, sending her only son to war was grossly unfair, and should only be considered when everyone else had already signed up themselves. I should be the last one in the country to join in.

My father sat quietly, in a chair in the corner of the kitchen, ignoring my mother's pleas to join in the rather one-sided debate.

He twizzled his stick in his hands, mulling things over, or reliving the nightmare. I couldn't quite tell.

He spoke quietly, but assertively, my mother sat down as he began to talk.

"He must go. It's his duty."

His tear-filled eyes looked up and met my mother's, whose tears had already begun racing to the ground.

The three of us sat there, frozen in a stunned silence in anticipation of what was to come.

"The boy more than likely won't see action anyway," he rasped reassuringly. I could tell he was lying, even if my mother didn't.

The sniffles grew weaker as my mother retreated upstairs, taking her sodden hanky with her. The floor-boards creaked gently as I heard her sit in the rocking chair that occupied the corner of their room.

"But, if you do, prepare yourself. It is hell on earth. Nothing will compare to it. You do not look out for your friends, you think you will, but you won't. It's all about survival."

Goosebumps rippled their way over my skin, a chill

sent straight up my spine, he had never spoken to me with such sincerity and foreboding in his voice before.

He withdrew a cigarette from his golden case, offered me one, which I declined, before he lit his. I felt uneasy, not because my Dad had uncharacteristically offered me one of his beloved cigarettes, but because of what he had said and how he had said it. He had never spoken to me in that way before, never with such seriousness and consequence as he had done in that moment. It made me question whether or not I had made the right decision by signing up, but it was too late to take it all back now, I didn't think the army would take too kindly to their newest recruit saying that he had made a mistake.

The path of his smoke twisted in the air and twirling, rose up, glided in the air for a moment, before dissipating into nothing.

We sat in silence, broken up only by Dad taking a short, sharp breath in, as if he was going to speak. Each time it came to nothing. Eventually, Dad finished his cigarette, before he grunted himself out of his chair and hobbled his way up the stairs.

3

The slow whooshing of wind passing over the wings continued incessantly as I began desperately throwing my head round in all directions, trying to spot our target. The wind was beginning to annoy me now, even though it was the very thing that was keeping us in the air at this moment, it was starting to distract me. I needed to be able to see our target and soon. I was growing increasingly impatient with everything that was out of my personal control.

We had to be perfect, there was no margin for error, we must land within a few hundred metres of our target. Anything more than that and we would render every man in the back of my craft completely useless.

They might as well be killed. The heavy burden that felt like it had been placed solely on my shoulders, was growing heavier and heavier by the second, dragging the Horsa closer and closer to the ground. My brain began to feel like it was pumping against the walls of my skull, as if it had replaced the role of my heart in pumping blood around my body.

I heard the heavy, wooden and uncooperative door behind me, slide open as the men cooped up behind, took a look at the ground below. I hoped that they would give us a hand in spotting our objective but knew that until we hit the ground, everything was down to me and my co-pilot. After all, they weren't the ones who had been given endless lessons on how to spot your landing site from this high up in a midnight sky. They were merely passengers in a very heavy object, gracefully falling to the ground.

Some of the boys were expecting children. Some were due quite soon whereas others had found out a few days before leaving. They had been overjoyed.

One by one they had received letters, insisted we should all head out, the pilots included, for a big booze up to celebrate. It would have been rude to say no, not to mention detrimental to their morale.

I wondered if they would ever see their children, some of them, I prayed earnestly, would get to see them grow up, but others, I was not a naïve person, would never see their home again, let alone their child.

I was not normally as negative as this, but the overwhelming tide of pessimism that drowned me was having a dangerous effect on me, it was like an Albatross around my neck, a millstone, that was slowly dragging me to the darkest depths of my own mind. I tried my best to flick my mind back to the task at hand. If I could help them land safely, and in the correct place, then maybe they would have a better chance at survival and getting back to their loved ones.

We knew the boys in our kite very well. We, like them, were new to gliders and so the majority of our training was carried out together. It was easy for us all to get along, we had all had our lives turned upside down by this war, and we were all determined to make the best of the situation that Herr Hitler had forced us all into. In some ways, we had become more like brothers since we had started training together, we had formed bonds that even some blood relatives would find it difficult to match. We knew each other's likes and dislikes, what wound them up and what their weaknesses were. But we also knew each other's strengths, what they would be best at when we were down on the ground and most importantly of all, that we could trust each other.

I'd watched with pride as the boys slowly gained more confidence in the glider, to the point where they could smoke, chat and sing. The silence that now engulfed them, and us, was harrowing. It was slowly becoming like the oxygen available in the Horsa was going scarce, the few mutterings that had been winding their way around the cabin, slowly drifting out into a nothingness, as the breathing inside became more laboured, more intense.

A few splutters from the men and the occasional creak as they shifted around was the only noise that emanated from behind me now. I began to feel tense for them, every muscle in my body cramping up slightly at the thought that within a few minutes, these boys would be in the deadly throes of combat, the slightest squeeze of a trigger all it would take for their lives to be stopped dead. I felt even worse when I suddenly remembered that I would be there with them.

What struck me was that I hadn't heard a single man vomit. On training, every one of them had vomited at some point or another, right up until our last training flight when the Captain regurgitated his breakfast for us all to inspect. The liquid, often watery and unsubstantial, would slosh its way over the deck of the aircraft, boots becoming soaked in the fluid, much to the disgust and annoyance of every trooper that would have to clean his boots as a consequence.

It was as if the fear, and the feeling of looking death straight in the face, had calmed them somehow. It was a notion that was advocated by many other, more experienced NCOs, particularly one Company Sergeant-Major who had taken it upon himself to give me a pep talk a few days before we left. It was of little use to me. For me, the anticipation of combat was rather overwhelming, something that I both wanted to get stuck in to and feared.

I thought of my father, of all those men sat in that church. They had done what was needed of them in their day, now it was time for me to do the same. I tried to conjure up some thought of what they might have said to themselves shortly before going over the top, or before they began digging out one of their mates from yet another collapsed trench tunnel, but I found it impossible. I only hoped that I would be able to summon up just enough inner strength to see me through, when the time came.

There was so much that could go wrong with our landing, I just prayed that we had released ourselves from the bomber at the correct moment. A lot hinged on that. Our training flights, often carried out under perfect conditions, were the prime examples of how something could quite easily take a turn for the worse. Not carrying out your pre-flight checks? That one had ended up with one co-pilot killed and his pilot chucked out of the army on medical grounds, after they had ended up buried in the side of a farmhouse. Miscalculating your speed? That one had caught out almost all of us, with one or two ending up with broken bones and more than a little bit of broken pride. We had to be perfect, we simply had to.

The pilot's briefing before take-off had not been as encouraging as I'd hoped on the brink of a big invasion. We knew it was coming, so we were all expecting a ravishingly uplifting and encouraging speech from our commanding officer about how we were all capable of heroics, in the face of the enemy, to carry out our duty and rid this small part of the world of tyranny. It was a moment that I had found myself strangely looking forward to, one that I was hoping that we would all be united in with cheers and rousing renditions of God Save the King.

I shuffled my grip on the controls and ignored the dryness of my mouth as I thought of what we had actually received in that tent at the side of that nondescript airstrip. It was not the rousing, Shakespearean speech that I had been expecting, but a sobering, joyless lecture on a new development that we would just have to accept.

Wooden poles, no, large wooden spikes, were being placed around our objective in an attempt to stop us from landing there.

I let out a sigh, sickened to the very pit of my stomach as I thought about what might happen if we were unlucky enough to strike one.

My co-pilot and I would be the first ones to be killed as the wooden shaft pierced its way through the flimsy plywood of the glider hitting the ground at speed. The entire craft would likely be split in two as it drove its way through, decimating anyone inside. I could feel myself wincing at the thought of being hit by one, the pain completely off the scale of what was imaginable to me.

The scene of carnage would be unbearable, I almost felt sorry for the enemy soldiers who had to clean up our mess.

Even if we didn't take a large spike to the face, one of the others might, and the noise alone would be enough to give away our position, and enough to raise the alarm before our slaughter. The only real option to me, to not be killed in pain by having a wooden spike buried into my skull, or being slowly tortured and killed by an enemy soldier, was to take my revolver, and press it against one of my temples, before we even landed. It was not the first time on this flight that I had entertained the thought, and it was only because of the effect upon my witnesses that I put the idea to bed.

The holes had been dug and ready for a few weeks now, I'd seen the photographs. I just prayed again that the stakes were not in yet. I prayed that the Germans, renowned for their engineering prowess and efficiency, had been more than just a little bit lazy when it came to the installation of the anti-glider poles.

I'd done a lot of praying in the last two hours, as if I felt closer to God being up in the sky. I wished I had listened in those church services now, maybe He would have been nicer to me if I had done.

Oh well, there was nothing I could do about that now.

Wiping my brow on my lower arm, I gripped the controls tighter.

4

The infantry had bored me, I'm ashamed to say it, but I couldn't stand the monotony of training runs, cleaning boots and rifle drill. There was nothing exciting about it, I wanted to be part of the war. That is what I had signed up for, it's what we all signed up for and yet, here we were, doing the same thing, day in, day out, with no real consequence. We were all itching to get stuck in, to actually apply our training to a real combat situation. We were all quite far down the naivety scale.

I knew I was safe where I was but the confidence I had gained from the other lads had made me want to push for more. I still kept myself to myself, but at the same time, when you're surrounded by that many, war-ready, like-minded young lads, there is no option but to come out of your shell and become just like one of them. I joined in with most of their recreational activities, but still tried to remain somewhat distant from them, and try not to damage the reputation that I had built up with my superiors.

I was a good soldier, in fact I'd been promoted, but I

was a bored one. I'd become a robot, a man with no emotions as I continuously carried out exactly what I was told to do. We were all slowly becoming bored, agitated, and it led to more than a few divisions within the regiment. I think that was part of our problem. We had all slowly become desensitised to the war, after spending hours upon hours of dreaming about it, all of us wanted to be somewhere but Britain, somewhere where there was something really kicking off, we wanted out of the monotony.

I'd even tried to get out of it. I'd put in a transfer request out to another regiment that was in the thick of it in North Africa. I was hauled in front of the CO who practically spat at me as he portrayed how much of a traitor I was to the regiment, but more importantly to my friends, he seemed to treat me like I had just urinated on his dead mother's grave.

"I wouldn't want you to be my platoon NCO in battle," he had hissed as I solemnly trudged out of his office.

A few months more of utter tedium and a call went up for men to join the Glider Pilot's Regiment, it was an opportunity that I simply had to take. I reasoned with myself that the CO would be far more willing to let me go this time, if they were actively seeking out recruits to go, surely he would have no choice but to sign the paperwork and let me leave. A few of the lads stuck their names down flippantly, like they had done with so many other pieces of paper that was bashed into the regimental noticeboard, not expecting to hear back from them again.

I'd never flown before, but the heroics of the Spitfire pilots was well documented. I had watched in awe and amazement as newsreel after newsreel showed little specks in the sky climbing and diving, banking and rolling as they bravely hunted down the enemy planes before blasting them out of the sky. I wanted a piece of that, even if it was just a slither of the respect that those pilots got from everyone around them. I wanted those wings on my chest, that was instantly recognised by anyone in the street and that would become associated with total courage and self-sacrifice. I needed to do it.

The feeling of floating in between the clouds, up where the sky is permanently blue, feeling the sun kiss your skin, was exactly what I wanted, what I yearned for. I wondered how similar it was to being a bird, silently floating around, seemingly with not a care in the world. I had spent hours watching the birds and marvelled at the way that they could skim through the air for a number of seconds, before having to propel themselves once again with their wings. I wondered how much like a bird a glider would be. I had no idea.

Shortly after, I had reported for training. I had excelled at learning to fly a plane, finishing close to top while others got the dreaded 'Return to Unit' notice letter. I felt sick at the thought of getting that letter, I would become a social outcast, the leper of my unit. I would be hated. It was almost an equal to the 'LMF' letter that was used in the Air Force and used as a threat which loomed over us for the entirety of our time in the army. Lack of Moral Fibre. Not something you'd want to have to explain to your mates.

It spurred me on further. I got on wonderfully with a plane with an engine, without an engine however, I was slightly unsure.

I loved every minute of it in fact. That feeling as the tow rope was detached for the very first time was something that I would never forget. I had looked at my co-pilot, the fear and terror in his eyes mirrored by my own. Nevertheless, we were both elated to finally be in this position and above all else, we managed to survive that first flight.

I was one of the first to complete my education on the training gliders and soon after, along with my co-pilot, was shipped off to an aerodrome to begin operational training.

The first time I saw a Horsa was like the first time I kissed a girl, exhilarating, but horrifically nerve-wracking at the same time. I ogled and marvelled at it for hours before getting inside it. It was all wooden, a massive structure with the biggest flaps possible, to the point that they didn't look like they should have been attached to the craft. The wings were huge, and they almost looked like a father who had his arms outstretched as his young child sped towards him. The proportions on it looked completely wrong and yet, it was beautiful.

I was infatuated with the thing. The one thing I almost couldn't bear was the fact that it would never be mine. It would belong to me momentarily as we softly descended through the sky but, after landing, it would be taken away never to be used again. In that respect, it was not like a plane at all.

Despite that, with every craft that I clambered into, boots thumping humorously on the flimsy wooden floor, I felt an instant, and loving connection with.

We flew countless training flights, predominantly with concrete blocks strapped to the seats that should have been occupied by soldiers. Maybe they didn't trust us just yet. The vigorous yanking of the tow plane, before a soft detachment of the tow rope, slowly became innate in us, to the point where it was part of our lives, like going to the toilet or sitting down for a meal.

Before long, we began to take real, living, breathing passengers. It was another one of those moments that I was slowly getting used to. I was utterly terrified, I had never been responsible for flying other people before, it was always just me and the co-pilot, but now, we were completely in control of these boys, we had their lives in our hands.

We began to get to know people, our tug crews introduced themselves to us and we frequently went out for a drink together. We started to form real, lasting bonds with the other people that would be part of our mission, when the time came. It was crucial, we all needed to know each other's strengths and weaknesses, so that we could operate at the pinnacle of our combined abilities.

Our boys in the back became more positive and confident with every landing, something that we were still learning. Gradually, the boys learned how to relax when they were in the back of our glider and for some, to even take it as a bit of downtime, resting their head on the man next to them and catching a few winks, or bringing a book along for the journey. Others, learned that they were able to smoke in the back of the Horsa, no matter what the official guidance had been, and on more than one occasion, someone had pulled out a mouth organ to serenade the others with, picking up a few voices along the way.

Just as we all got used to this however, we were issued with strange, tinted goggles that we began to wear on our training landings. They turned the brilliant light of day into a strange dullness meant to be night.

None of us dared take them off, if we were going to

have to land at night, we'd need to train as close to the real thing as possible.

Before long, we had the concrete blocks for passengers again as we came down time after time in total darkness. A potential landing at night was not something that I was comfortable with at all, how were we to get everything right if we could see next to nothing? As the weeks wore on, I felt like our officers were beginning to ask slightly too much of us.

The training for us pilots was more rigorous than the boys in the back, I thought. We trained on our kites, in navigation, in communications and also as a light infantry soldier. None of us complained though, we had signed up for it, this is what we had wanted. Every single one of us in the GPR were driven, hardworking individuals and the intense training and fitness regimen suited us all down to the ground. We weren't going to give this opportunity up. We had a tough time, but we were the celebrities on base.

The controls became second nature to us, the Horsas our best friends, our passengers became accustomed.

We were ready.

5

A small pin prick of brilliant white light poked its way through the darkness that shrouded the cockpit. The torch was masked with tape, allowing the most minute bit of light out, the rest trying desperately to force its way out, making the tape glow menacingly. I had appreciated his efforts to keep his light concealed in the best way he could, not because I believed we could be spotted by that stream of light, but because the burst of light, when the tape was not around it, was enough to make me squint and cause a decent headache.

I watched him as he worked, the stream of light gliding its way over the map in front of him before changing course over towards the face of his stopwatch. The map had all sorts of scribbles and pencil markings all over it, most of which I could not make out in the darkness. I could see though, where our flight path had been plotted, a solid pencil line, that had been run over itself many times, signalling the exact points where my co-pilot would issue instructions to me.

The moonlight was good, but not quite good enough for my co-pilot, but not many things were up to his standard apparently, including me. We had struggled to get on at first, both of us making it quite clear what we thought about the other and that it was only because we had to fly together that we were even talking to each other.

I tried not to get too attached to my co-pilot, as we had been instructed, and at first it seemed easy enough for me to keep my distance. But spending that much time with one person tends to have the opposite effect to what our superiors wanted.

I knew why they wanted us to remain distant, in case one of us was killed, or worse, binned off the course, and out of the regiment altogether. We couldn't afford to have pilots moping around because their best mate had been returned to his unit. We needed to be able to lose someone in the morning and have wiped them from our memories by the evening. However, over time I had got to know my co-pilot, it was inevitable, we began seeking each other out in the mess before plonking our behinds down next to each other and tucking into another string-filled casserole.

He adored the food that we were served, whereas I found it was something that I would only eat for the simple reason that I had to. It made me wonder about what sort of impoverished lifestyle he had come from before, which meant that he thought he was dining at the Ritz. He had an almighty appetite, often eating everything on his plate as well as anything left over on anyone else's. He was a frequent visitor to the NAAFI, even offering to go for other people in return for a small cut of the goods that he picked up for them. It was a business venture that never fully took off, but he was often seen around the base tucking in to some exotic food he had traded with the Yanks.

I often teased him that we would have to be careful on operations as we would need to account for his weight, and I was glad when the notice for this operation came through when it did, as news had just reached us that the NAAFI had taken a consignment of American chocolate bars. If we were leaving a day or two later, it would have allowed him a lot more time to stock up on what he liked to call the 'Nectar of the Allies.'

His pockets were stuffed almost immediately, and I was quite sure that if he turned out his pockets now, more than one bar would be residing in them, probably all half eaten.

John 'Johnny' Chambers was a Cockney, a proper rough, East End lad, and he was proud of it. He was a good friend to have, never taking rubbish from anyone and although he loved American delicacies, he wasn't too keen on the Americans themselves, being known on more than one occasion to throw a solid fist towards the nose of one of our cousins. His run ins with the Americans was an issue that I never had and had found that they were a perfect compliment to the British Army, with their sense of humour and courage. Maybe that's why Johnny hadn't liked them, he saw them as competition, as a threat.

Johnny wasn't scared of anyone though, or it seemed anything, always acting in the calmest way possible, which was strange for a nineteen-year-old boy. I did begin to ponder how he would feel as the tow rope was detached on our first operational mission. As the days had ticked by and the hours counted down to take off, he had slowly drawn into himself, not his usual outlandish, loud self. I just hoped that whatever was going through his mind right now, wouldn't affect his abilities to guide us in towards our target.

Generally, he was a light-hearted soul, which had made his protests against his nickname far more amusing to us than it should have been. He hadn't liked the pet name of 'baby face' one bit, but his objections to it made it stick all the more and so that is how he was affectionately known.

I looked at his face in the silvery light of the moon and the orange glow of torchlight and marvelled at how smooth his skin really was, it really did make his nickname seem all the more appropriate, especially the longer I looked at him. It was like a desert, no real features of major importance but still something that seemed remarkable.

Not a single hair ever protruded from his chin, either a sign of incredible personal hygiene and discipline, or a true indicator of how young these boys really were.

I wasn't much older than Johnny, but I was still coined 'Grandad' as I was the oldest glider pilot on base. I didn't mind too much, in fact I felt quite honoured to even be considered worthy of a nickname, I'd never really got close enough to anyone before to be labelled with one.

His eyes were trained intently on the focus of the torchlight, never blinking, his vision reserved solely for his stopwatch. I fought with all the urges in my body, trying to take my eyes away from him for a moment, it wasn't my job to be looking at the stopwatch and I knew I could trust Johnny to make sure that our final run-in was at exactly the right time.

I watched as the second hand ticked round silently, John making a mental note of how long we had been released for. I knew to not interrupt him when we were on this stage, if I made him get it wrong, I didn't just kill myself, but I would also kill the thirty odd elite soldiers in the back. He was in his zone, he was completely focused. If you were to see him outside of a glider, you wouldn't have thought it was capable for a boy like him to sit still for so long, or for him to be able to stare at a map and stopwatch in the dark as intently as he was.

All that training, would be for nothing.

I loosened my grip on the wooden controls before gripping them tightly again, making sure the blood supply to my hands was still good, and they didn't cramp up at the most crucial moment, the slightest thing, the simplest, would be all it took for me to lose control of the Horsa and end up killing us all.

My hands were cold, as was my whole body, but a film of sweat had settled over every inch of my palms, making them feel like the controls could slip out of my grasp at any moment.

My stomach churned violently and gurgled as the seconds began to tick by slower on John's stopwatch. He still hadn't blinked.

I scratched at my ear, trying to flick out any dirt that may be laying there, so that I could hear everything that was going on. I tilted my head slightly so that I didn't miss the shout from my co-pilot.

I knew I wouldn't miss it, John had one of the loudest, clearest and most recognisable voices in the entire regiment. It was one of those voices that had the capability of landing him in hot water, even if he was just saying 'Good morning' to one of the Lieutenants. It wasn't that he wasn't liked by his superiors, but they just didn't like lads like him. He was working class, a Cockney and he was brilliant at his job. Just like Johnny saw the Americans as a bit of a friendly threat, so too did the officers when they realised how good at his role John Chambers truly was.

Normally he wouldn't shut up, right now though, he wasn't saying a word.

I waited for his signal.

6

I was the oldest in our group of pilots, not by much, eighteen months at the most, but I was still the least confident and went into myself at most opportunities. Although I tried my hardest to be like all of the others, it was difficult for me, like I had some sort of physical barrier that was stopping me from just stepping over that boundary and being properly accepted. John seemed to be the only one who was truly prepared to leap over that boundary for me.

Our first night of leave after completing our training was spent near to base as we'd all agreed to go out to a dance together before our next phase of training began. It was a welcome bit of downtime, something that we had been lusting after for weeks now. It wasn't just breaking the cycle of training flights and fitness work, but it meant that it would be the first time that we headed out together, off base, like a group of normal young lads should.

I ended up sitting with John, nursing a half pint and rolling the glass around the table, I had never been much of a drinker and found it difficult to stomach the taste of the stuff that they served in that hall. My opposition to the taste and my tendency not to drink however, didn't mean that John and I hadn't ended up in a few funny situations together as a result of alcohol, but it was something I could neither remember or want to be reminded of. John didn't much like going to these dances, he already had a girl-friend back home and didn't like the idea of even looking at another girl, so spent much of his night looking down the bottom of his glass.

Circling like vultures as soon as we had stepped through the door, the others had muttered to one another about who they would like to claim for the evening, and the ground rules for if one of them took a fancy to someone else. They had spotted their prey almost immedi-ately, and had moved in shortly afterwards, leaving the girls, some more petrified than a small field mouse, with little choice but to pair off with them for the night.

I did not care for such barbarity when it came to searching for a mate, it did not suit me, nor did I want to find a partner in that way. I very often ended up leaving the dance with John, who drunkenly hummed or screamed songs at the top of his voice as we headed back to base, with nothing more than a dull headache after listening to the incessant music at the table.

John nudged me and nodded his head in the direction of the door and we headed outside together to gain a brief respite from the music.

He whipped out his cigarette holder and twizzled one in between his fingers before sticking it in his mouth. He then turned the open box to me, the mirrored gold reflecting the moonlight onto my face.

He knew I didn't smoke, but he always offered me one,

whether it was some kind of joke to him I didn't know, but he just couldn't seem to help himself.

We stood in silence as the smoke spiralled its way into the night sky, intertwining with other streams of smoke from around us. I'd never understood the fascination with constantly having to have a cigarette, it meant having to stand around waiting for someone to finish puffing away before being able to have a decent conversation with them. It also meant that a good deal of your pay was already earmarked for the purpose before you'd even seen a shilling of it, I could never get my head around it. Still, it didn't stop me from dutifully following John outside so that I could suck in some of the relatively fresh air, while he took in his smoke-filled oxygen.

The sun had just dipped behind the trees that marked the horizon, the landscape around us basking in the vibrant orange of a setting sun, as if it had set fire to the fields in the distance as a last, fleeting action for the day.

"We'll be up there soon, mate," he said longingly.

"Your old man was in the first one, wasn't he?" John broke the silence again, deeming the conversation far too unimportant to take his eyes from the cigarette that he was rolling around in between his fingers. I couldn't quite bring myself to answer straight away, it was like something was holding me back, almost as if I had forgotten who my Dad was, and I was trying to rack my brain to remember.

The village hall was quite a nice one here, untouched by German bombs, the hall opened out onto the village green, where a small pond had been added to commemorate the loss of life in the first war.

The water was stagnant and had a thick layer of

mildew on it, the fish, who I was told used to live in there, had died years ago. In that moment, I found myself longing to have been in this village before the war began, so that I could take in the fish serenely slithering through the water, with no care in the world.

"Yeah, lied about his age too." Our conversation ended abruptly, as we let the slow beat from the music infiltrate our ears once more, beckoning us in, as it did with a large crowd who were also standing out on the green with us.

He flicked his cigarette across the green, almost reaching the pond and we both took that as the signal to take a slow walk back into the hall, I noticed that a few others had started to do the same. Obviously, the music was drawing to its finale and no one wanted to miss their last opportunity to find someone to couple off with.

As we shuffled in reluctantly, I took a look around, catching the gaze of a girl. I did a double take as I found myself in utter shock that someone had been looking at me, especially in the way that she had.

We looked at each other briefly, a sweet smile flicked across her face which I returned, but I quickly found my face burning up and turning a bright shade of red. I held her gaze a moment longer before trotting to catch up with John, not wanting to risk the only real friendship I had for a random girl.

She was quite small, probably only coming up to my chest if we stood side by side but had something about her where I knew her presence regardless of her size. She looked around the same age as me, maybe a year younger at twenty or twenty-one, at least I desperately hoped that she was. It seemed like we had something immediately, there was a mutual attraction as we kept our gaze fixed upon one another.

She had wildly green eyes, which I seemed to lose myself in completely in that brief moment that I shared with her. They had a seriousness about them, a fieriness that I longed to know more about, but they were also kind, loving eyes, the kind that immediately set you at ease, like a mother's.

In those eyes, I could see everything I'd ever dreamed of, an entire future of two people who would never meet again.

Her skin was soft and smooth, her cheeks a brighter shade of pink to the rest of her, making her smile seem warmer and more inviting somehow. She continued to draw me in, more than the music had ever done and I felt myself having to resist walking after John, just so that I could keep my eyes on her for a few moments more.

She wore a pale pink, floral dress that flapped around her shins as she stood in the gentle breeze of the English countryside, a pair of faded green gloves and small handbag completing her outfit.

I'd never before taken this much notice of what a girl was wearing.

I'd only looked at her for a short time, maybe two seconds, but she was ingrained in my mind, I couldn't shake her. She was like a fly in my brain that night, buzzing around in my head, refusing to leave. My mind was shaken, like someone had given it a jolly good battering and one that prevented all other thoughts from entering my consciousness. I was aware John was talking to me, but what he was saying was muffled, indecipherable to me as I became intoxicated on my memory of the girl.

I saw the back of her as she left the dance early, I'd missed my chance.

Soon after, I made my excuse to Johnny and, obligingly, he came back with me to the base.

"You're quiet tonight mate," he said in between anecdotal stories of childhood stealing and bust ups.

I had nothing to say, I felt miserable that the only girl I'd ever felt a connection with had left, I'd never see her again. I'd never get that future with her and all we'd got was a momentary look at each other.

Like a mischievous teenager sneaking in stinking of booze, the Captain snuck up on us silently. The first we knew of his presence was when he spoke. He had an almost brilliant knack of coming up to talk to us at the exact moment that we needed to focus our entire attention on the Horsa, never when we were being towed and had a slightly less strenuous task on our hands.

His accent was rounded and he spoke well, enunciating every letter. His voice was normally soft and calm, raising his voice only when he needed to, but tonight it was strained, tense.

"How much longer, gents?"

It was so strained in fact, that it sounded like he was a little child, bursting to use the nearest toilet but knowing that there wouldn't be one available for a considerable amount of time.

He knew exactly how much longer it was, he'd been on all the training missions that we'd done a hundred times before. To be fair to him, I don't think it was just him that had the worst timing possible, it had seemed that all the officers we had taken with us during training, had all possessed the innate ability to want to distract us at the most crucial time possible. I don't think they had a sense of danger, or a sense of their own mortality, as they seemed to care little for ours and that of their men each time they distracted us.

His breath was still clean, he hadn't thrown up so far tonight. But there was still time for him to let his nerves get the better of him. It was unfortunate that he had been fairly consistent in showing us his breakfast on all our previous flights, especially as he was an officer and that the lads in the back were particularly brutal. His unofficial nickname had become 'Captain Sicknote' or simply 'CapSick.'

He had no reason for asking, he was just a terrible passenger, he needed to be in control at all times. A few of the non-commissioned lads were the same, but they weren't able to get up and walk around, trying to examine the situation and exert some control, as they were hollered at as soon as they moved so much as a bum cheek.

"Sit down!" I barked, not thinking of the possible consequences.

I could sense John smirking as I did it, he felt exactly the same as me. He would know soon enough how long it was, as long as he was sitting down in his safe position rather than standing up when we hit the deck. If he was, he would shoot in between John and me, and straight out of the cockpit window. It felt good, two lowly staff sergeants being in charge of an officer, being able to shout orders to a Captain, especially one who was about twenty years our senior.

Being a young man and being able to tell an older man off, gives such an overwhelming sense of power and jurisdiction that made me feel invincible. I decided there and then that I would go for a commission when I made it home, I could get quite used to bossing people around and telling them what to do.

The extra money and better food was also a bonus too. Maybe John should consider it, he could buy more chocolate.

While we were in the air, we were in charge of everyone, including the Captain. As soon as we'd landed on the ground though, we were soldiers, the Captain would resume control of us and probably make us suffer for my outburst. Being in charge of everyone, was not something that sat comfortably with me, it wasn't a natural position for me to be in. I was not a natural leader, I had the ability to think like an officer, but to lead men was a thought so daunting I rarely entertained the prospect. John on the other hand, would make a fantastic leader one day, I was sure of it.

As I thought about what lay ahead once we hit the ground, I took a tighter grip on the wooden control with my left hand and pushed my right hand down the side of my seat. I would become a soldier, as soon as the Horsa came to a standstill. My dream of becoming a warrior was about to be realised and I couldn't have been more terrified.

I felt comforted as I felt the cold steel of my Sten gun, loaded and ready to fire the second we touched down. I had gone against the recommendations of an older Company Sergeant Major I had met, who claimed that on landing in the glider, it was possible that the Sten would discharge all of its rounds. I discarded the comment as a myth and, even if it was the truth, I thought it would shorten my torment of being in the middle of a war zone. I only hoped we'd make it long enough to use it.

The fortified silence was interrupted by boots thumping their way back down the aircraft as the Captain skulked back to his seat remorsefully.

I didn't feel sorry for him, he didn't have to wait long after being released to do his job, all he needed to do was let us do ours, then everything would be over to him, he would resume total control.

The pin prick of light that illuminated the cockpit in a dull orange suddenly flicked off, subjecting us to the darkness of the night once more. All of a sudden, I felt like I was lost without the light, as if that was what was keeping me sane, it was my only comfort. We were back in the more familiar darkness, but this time it was an uneasy one, one that made me feel like I would never have clear thoughts ever again.

The stopwatch was packed away hastily and rather noisily before the compass was slotted in gracefully into John's breast pocket. That was it, all of his utensils were gone now, it was just us two, the flimsy controls and the goodwill of the men in the back that would be guiding us down to the drop zone. This was it. Everything we had trained for, everything we had waited for, would come down to the next few seconds.

He looked across at me, his impossibly soft face almost reflecting the moonlight of it and shining onto mine like a mirror. He was maintaining a calm exterior that I refused believe was being repeated on the inside of his mind, or maybe it was just me, maybe I was the only glider pilot who was almost paralytically fearful of what was about to happen.

His eyes seemed to glow as he excitedly shifted in his chair, he was really fired up. The quivering in his hand was all but gone and a new bravery had poured over him.

"Go."

I took the controls and sent the plane into a steep dive as John fumbled around strapping on his helmet.

"You have control."

"I have control," came his acknowledgment.

I plonked my helmet on my head. It was a standard paratrooper's helmet, the same as all the men in the back. When we landed, we looked identical to them, we fought the same as them, we just had a little extra responsibility beforehand.

It was a dark khaki, pretty uncomfortable to wear, and had a mesh netting pulled over the surface of it.

If I felt like it, I could pull some foliage out of my surroundings and attach it to the mesh, making me blend in a little more and avoid being sniped at.

That was the theory anyway, but when the foliage growing around the target was moss and mould, I thought I'd pass.

How a little bit of green would camouflage me against the backdrop of a huge steel bridge was beyond me.

I pulled the strap on tight, to the point where it had begun pinching the skin. It wasn't comfortable, in fact it couldn't have been more uncomfortable, but at least I knew it would stay on when my head inevitably crashed into the wooden structure around me.

"Brace for impact!" I didn't recognise my own voice, in fact, it had barely registered with me that I had even shouted anything, I was completely on autopilot now, the training and retraining taking hold of me so that I barely had to think through what I was doing.

The sound of boots thudding as they slotted comfortably on the benches in front of them, forming a rather amusing looking tunnel throughout the back of the aircraft thumped its way to my ears.

Their arms would be linking with one another simultaneously, they would become one body all holding onto each other for safety, and not just for the landing. A wave of jealously took hold of me, a part of me that wished to be able to link arms with the boys in the back. I began to feel isolated, desperately alone, even though I had John by my side.

Our speed began to pick up as we lost a dramatic amount of height.

Our invasion was about to begin.

8

Our wedding day was amazing. It had been a quick decision really, but I knew it was the right one. We'd been on a few dates after the dance; cinema, walks, that sort of thing and from there everything blossomed.

That first kiss was everything, it was all I could think about for weeks afterwards, I just wanted to see her again so we could recreate that moment. We'd walked for an hour or two around the fields and hills surrounding the base and sat down on the top of the hill that overlooked the town.

It was a perfectly blue day, not a single cloud in the sky, a perfect day for flying. The sky was a brilliant shade of blue and we sat, hands behind us, propping ourselves up and marvelled at it.

The sky was mesmerising as we observed bird after bird, flap by, swooping down into the village. The weather was clear, but still chilly. The February air was biting, biting in particular at Christine's arms, her light hairs pricking up and catching the breeze.

I threw my jacket around her shoulders as we walked back down the hill, my arms clamping the jacket down as it flapped in the wind.

She stopped and turned to face me, and as we kissed my grip loosened on my jacket and it began to slide off.

"Too cold to not have this on," she chuckled as she bolted down the hill yanking me along by the hand.

I proposed at the bottom of that hill.

I don't know what made me do it, I felt compelled to. I had no ring, no romantic speech like an American movie, I had nothing but raw emotion. The strange thing was, I hadn't regretted my decision in the slightest.

I'd fallen in love in that brief momentary glance at the dance, the smile that she gave me was one that made me dream of a future and now, that future seemed one step closer to reality.

The wedding was small, in her church in the town. My family made it as well as hers and after introducing themselves to each other, the vows were exchanged.

My mother sacrificed her wedding ring so Christine was able to have one for the day, we would replace it in a few months' time, hopefully when the war would be nearing an end.

I wore my uniform, it was easier that way, and cheaper. The other boys from the regiment provided a guard of honour for us as we ecstatically walked out the church.

Christine wore a plain white dress, with a small rose attached to her chest, she looked the most beautiful that I had ever seen her.

She wore a simple veil, one that she preferred to keep swept back, leaving her face uncovered. That veil now sat proudly on the window ledge of our home, making sure that all the passers-by knew that we were newlyweds.

We had a week-long honeymoon in Bournemouth, a luxury provided by Christine's father, and we spent the week cooped up in a small chalet on the coast, enjoying the British September rainfall. We didn't mind though.

We spent every day outside as if it was unbearably hot, as long as we had each other's company, it didn't matter what the rest of the world, including the weather, was doing.

I was one of the fortunate one's on base. I had my wife and now my home nearby and so I was able to sneak home to my wife on an evening pass.

Shortly before Christmas, I cycled my way off the base, bid a cheerio to the sentry, and headed home.

Christine was sat by the door, fire roaring, waiting for me. I loved our little home, it wasn't much to look at, but it was ours, our own little safe haven where the war and other people didn't matter, they wouldn't disturb us here.

She occupied the wing backed chair by the door, seemingly just sitting there; no newspaper or book in her hand, no knitting while listening to the wireless churning out overly upbeat music or droning newsreaders. She just sat, in silence. She didn't even bother to say 'Hello' to me, instead opting to launch into whatever she had been bottling up for the whole day.

"I went out today," her eyes began filling with tears and she tried breathing in between little sobs. My mind began spinning at an immeasurable speed at what may have happened to make her react in this way. I thought maybe that her brother had been killed or something to do with her mother's health perhaps, but no words slipped out of her mouth.

Throwing my beret on to the table, I lurched towards her and gave her a hug. We held our position for what felt like an age and I began to make myself feel sick with worry and in anticipation of what she might eventually say.

She broke the hug and looked into my eyes, with a wry smile spread across part of her face.

"We're having a baby," she sobbed, and squeezed me tight, burying her head into my chest.

I stood, open mouthed for a moment, blinking several times, double checking I was still awake.

I began to wheeze, which turned in to a wheezy sort of laugh. Tears streaming down my face now too, we stood for an hour or two in our front room, giggling and chuckling to each other.

I was going to be a father, I couldn't quite get my head around it, a smaller version of me, fused with my favourite person in the world, would be joining us. It was such a crazy thought, an overwhelming prospect, that I could barely think straight, I could hardly imagine what my life would be like when I had a new primary concern in my life.

I sobbed for days afterwards. In between my sobbing, the boys took me out for a drink, it was a ritual that all the expectant fathers were forced to go through whether they wanted to do it or not. It was a ceremony that was enjoyed by all ranks, and on a few occasions after my happy news, we had taken some of the junior officers out with us, soon after they had received similar news. As we headed home from the evening out, with more than my fair share of alcohol festering in my body I realised something. Something that I knew already but one that in an alcohol enlightened mind, seemed to mean something more than it would have done if I was sober. I had joined the group of men who had wives and girlfriends expecting.

I couldn't believe it.

Then the due date came through.

The sixth of June 1944.

9

Although we were hurtling towards the ground at one hundred miles an hour, the lives of many men in the back, many who were married, some expecting children of their own, I could not get the thought of my own family out of my head.

All leave was cancelled, even for those whose wives' were expecting that very week. All communication was restricted, only that was considered of paramount importance to the upcoming mission was granted.

I wasn't going to know before we left whether my wife was going to have a little boy or a little girl. She may have already given birth, there was no way of me knowing.

I thought of Christine, alone in our house, preparing to give birth without her husband. She would be in such pain and I wouldn't be the first person she would see on the other side of that pain. I felt incredibly depressed at the thought, and for every second that I thought about it, my limbs seemed to get heavier.

I sighed at the prospect of other people getting to hold

my child before their father held them. I longed to be there, waiting till the early hours before being told I was allowed in. I fantasised over it several times in the matter of days I had to stew over my own emotions and frustrations.

I wanted to be the first man to pick up my baby girl or little boy and cradle them for hours, talking to them, letting them know how lucky they truly were to have such a loving, caring and beautiful person like their mother.

I needed to see Christine, to tell her how proud I was of her, of how far we'd come together already and tell her how much I loved her. She needed to know that even if I wasn't coming back, I had our future mapped out already, every little detail and that it was just this war that had paused all of that.

I always kept my letters from Christine in my inside pocket, but tonight, we had no identification, nothing that could give away who we were, where we were from or what we would go on to do. Hopefully, if all went to plan, we would be sent home in a few weeks in readiness for the next time our services were required.

I tapped my inside pocket as a gesture, a comfort to me that she was always there with me, my real co-pilot.

I would explain to my child about their father, how he was an utterly useless man, who forgot birthdays, anniversaries and barely remembered to feed himself. I just wanted an opportunity to explain to them why their father wasn't there to greet them into the world and that he would try his best to get to see them as quickly as he could.

I dreamed about being the one to teach them to read and write, I would take hours out of my day to do it, or give up working just to spend extra time with them.

The future that I had seen in that young girl's eyes at that dance was happening, but it was all happening in my head. It was going to occur without me.

The more I thought about my absence at the birth of my child, the more I thought about the possibility of my permanent absence. This was another thing we had been instructed not to do, but it is only natural for a man to think about the things he loves most in life, in the face of death.

I knew I was in the same situation as every man in this plane, and the other two that flew by our sides, but I couldn't feel compassion for them, I had my own feelings to worry about.

I found myself praying again, praying that I would at least do my job to the best of my ability and, if it was God's plan, to lead me to the other side to watch my child grow up, like a normal father.

To make totally sure that God would hear my prayer, I would need to play my part. I needed to focus wholeheartedly on what I was about to do, and not place my life, or the lives of those in my plane, in jeopardy.

I needed to forget about my family.

I pushed them to the back of my mind.

10

I wrestled with my wooden, oversized, overweight bird as it plummeted to the ground. I tried in earnest to keep the plane airborne for as long as possible, preventing gravity from taking its inevitable victim just yet.

Trees became visible as we raced past, much too quickly for my liking, they were all merged into one great blur as they zipped past my windows, threatening to bring down the whole aircraft with a glancing blow.

John and I sat in total silence now, struggling and sweating to bring down our craft at the correct landing site.

I could sense a few pairs of eyes behind us boring into the back of my head as they watched intently as these two men, responsible for all their lives, fought with a force of nature to stop a speeding log from killing them all.

I swore I could also hear a few prayer beads clicking in between someone's hands, a few of the lads had had them on the training flights, as they rasped out the Lord's Prayer or Hail Mary's or whatever they wanted as we moved closer to hell.

Suddenly, our target appeared at our eleven o'clock, as if someone had suddenly plonked it there, John needlessly pointing it out to me as we scurried towards it.

Its tall, imposing, grey structure looked odd over the rest of the landscape. The futuristic design of the bridge somehow didn't fit in with the rest of the aesthetics of the village, as it somehow glowed in the moonlight.

The moon lit up everything that I needed to see. I could see where we were about to pitch down for the night, still coming in way too fast.

The frame of the plane creaked like I'd never heard it before as it wrestled with the speed and the way in which I was forcing it to stay airborne much longer than it wanted to. This Horsa had been put to work, it had done well, it was my favourite one yet.

Just a few more seconds Horsey, just give me a few more.

I willed it to give me more time, as if I was on a marathon, in the last straight, ready to give up. I found myself rocking backwards and forwards trying to give it a physical helping hand, pushing closer and closer to the finishing line.

It kept going for a few seconds more.

As I grunted and strained, I felt the nervous faces behind me, darkened by the paint smeared across them, all stare at me, praying for me.

We still had the speed, but we didn't have the height, I would start to see the individual grass blades before too long.

The river was now racing past us on the left, the glistening moonlight bouncing off it and flashing around my eyes. I tilted my head slightly so as to avoid the glare, the thing I needed the least right now was a headache, I already had one of those.

"Too fast!" I shouted like an absolute mad man, "we're going to need the chute!"

John grunted some sort of reply, but it was too late now if he was actually disagreeing with me. If we didn't use the chute, we would plough straight into our target, which wouldn't exactly be ideal at one hundred miles an hour.

John readied himself.

I fixed my gaze across the river now and watched as the tower loomed closer towards us, I would hold my breath from now on.

The water tower passed us, quickly.

I let the wheels of the Horsa just kiss the French countryside, trimming just the very tops of the daisies that I imagined to be there. A low, soft rumble echoed around the cabin as they slipped and slid over the cold surface.

"Stream!"

I was a machine, I had no emotions now, just doing what was necessary.

Johnny released the chute out of the back and instantly I preferred the option of clattering into tonnes of heavy steel at speed.

The chute deployed and lifting the back end of the craft back into the air, like a child lifting a mouse up by its tail, my head was sent flying forwards as the rest of my body seemed to want to go backwards.

John didn't need any instruction, he jettisoned the chute immediately and as we slid along the ground on our belly, there was nothing else I could do but become a passenger as we ground to a halt.

We scraped over rocks with an almighty racket and

sparks began to spray up in every direction as our bodies seemed to convulse with the rocking.

I felt every bump as we crashed over the holes where the anti-glider poles should have been, I made a mental note to thank God for that one.

I let out a sigh of relief, almost followed by a torrent of vomit, which I suppressed.

After a steady hissing as we glided over the ground, silence ensued once more.

We had come to a halt. No gunfire, no shouting, no guns pointing in our faces as we sat helplessly in our beloved wreckage. Just total silence.

The invasion had begun.

THE END

'ALL MEN ARE CASUALTIES' SAMPLE

All Men are Casualties is the second book in the 'Gliders over Normandy' series - read on for a sample of Chapter 1!

1

6th June 1944
00.16 hours

My head pounded, and my spine felt as if it was being stretched as I began to come round. I arched my back in earnest trying to realign my body and subdue some of the pain.

My chin was tucked into my chest and my arms felt heavy as they drooped limply down by my sides. A dull ache emanated from them as blood was reintroduced, a pulsating feeling as it was pumped round my limbs.

Everything seemed in total darkness.

My eyes were heavy as I tried desperately to take in as much information as I could. My cockpit was ruined, the windscreen had vanished, my controls had been eaten up by a mixture of bushes and barbed wire, and my seat creaked as it clung precariously to the main body of the aircraft.

I sucked in a mouthful of air sharply, as I tried to regain my normal levels of consciousness. Slowly, reluctantly, I began to lift my head. It was heavy with the added weight of a helmet and as I undid the straps, letting it fall into my lap, a large dent was clearly visible in the centre, where I had collided with the solid structure around me.

The darkness was captivating and it took me a few seconds of adjustment before I could begin to make out the outlines of objects around me.

Warm liquid began to run over my left eye and as I wiped it away discovered that I had a small crater in my head, just on the hairline, that was flowing down slowly like an obstructed waterfall. I plugged the gap momentarily with my index finger, in the same way that a leaky pipe, spurting water everywhere would be stemmed.

Brushing my hair over the wound, I pushed a clump into the hole, feeling it soak up the moisture almost immediately. I let it cling to my head, allowing it to stop the flow of blood from dripping down into my eyes.

My ears had popped, and I tried to clear them desperately by pinching my nose hard and blowing violently, putting so much pressure on my brain that it felt as if it would burst from my skull. Nothing worked, I was temporarily deaf.

My neck creaked and cracked as I commanded enough energy to lift my weary head and look around me. I allowed myself a quick roll of my skull, my vertebrae popping with each degree that I rotated.

As I looked over to my left, it took a moment or two for me to realise what I was seeing. I felt my eyes narrow and expand as my brain struggled to register the simplest information. The seat where my pilot, Charlie Manning, should be sat, was no longer there. The wooden floor where his chair should have been firmly housed, was completely bare, except for a series of large gouges running along towards the controls.

Desperate to not let the invasion begin without me, I began unbuckling myself, yanking and snatching at the clutches of the Horsa. She had been a faithful craft up till this point but now I had a different job to do, she would have to let me go.

My ears slowly began to tune back in to the environment I was in and I stopped as I tried to make out an unusual noise. My jaw hung open and my breathing ceased as I willed whatever it was to echo again.

A low rumble was coming from straight in front of me, I couldn't tell what it was. I cocked my head to one side, so the noise could hit my ear more directly, hoping earnestly that I would be able to decipher the moan from in front of me. As the midnight breeze drifted over the field, a low, constant hiss carried more audible sounds to my awaiting ear.

The groan intensified from a quiet breathing to a more determined grunt. Silence ensued.

Then, a cough.

"Johnny."

I still couldn't get my head around it, a few moments after, a plea rasped out once more.

"Johnny, get me out of here," he was Home Counties, not quite a Rupert, but not your East End Cockney that I had been blessed with. It was an accent that I had never experienced until I met him, it was an accent of some far away society, reserved only for royalty or the newsreader on the wireless.

The silence that engulfed his speech was haunting. I heard no shuffles, no swaying of bushes or snapping of twigs. Not even any gunshots. Just total, deathly silence.

"Come on John, you there, mate?"

"Yeah, I'm here, give me a minute."

I wasn't entirely sure if my reassurance was as convincing as I'd hoped. Fiddling around in my breast pocket, I found the small torch that I had for navigation, it was a funny looking thing, given to me by an American back at base in exchange for a taste of some corned beef, I'd come away from that particular transaction feeling very proud of myself.

The torch was heavy, in a sort of L shape, and flicking the switch on the side gave a small orange glow to the surrounding area, made smaller by the tape I'd filled most of the glass with, to restrict the potential target I'd become. Its pinprick of light wavered and shook slightly as I directed it towards the noise, and I used my free hand to grip my wrist to steady myself. Shutting my eyes momentarily, I breathed heavily, trying to compose myself and let the nausea pass.

Charlie was lying face down in a bush, still strapped in faithfully to his chair. He looked like a lost little boy. His arms and legs were flailing outwards, as if he was paddling to keep himself afloat. It served no purpose here, all he was achieving was tangling himself up in weeds and scratching himself on thorns.

My head pounded almost in unison with my heart. I shut my eyes for a second and let the stinging sensation die down.

For a moment, I was back home. Watching my brother as he dangled from a tree by his arm, clinging on for his life. He screamed and hollered at me to help him, but I was too far away. He was out of my reach.

I needed to help him, he wanted me to save him, it was my job, my *duty* to stop my younger brother from coming to harm.

I stared at him, knowing with absolute certainty that he was about to be hurt. He was high up, the best he could hope for would be a broken leg, and all manner of other injuries besides.

The branch was too weak though, it was already creaking and straining under his considerably lighter load, if I was to clamber across, we would both end up falling.

He had done well to hold himself where he was, he had slipped higher up and managed to clamp himself to the branch he now clung to.

Blood dripped intermittently from the bottom of his chin. It had rolled from a wound just under his eyebrow and trickled slowly like a lake rippling in a gentle breeze. I was fixated with the droplet as it began to cling loosely to his face before leaping to the ground. That single droplet of scarlet fluid had brought me so much peace, so much tranquillity, that I began to question why it had brought so much serenity to me.

He began to cry. Even he, with his unquestioning trust in me, knew his situation was helpless. The branch began to crack and all I could do was watch as he plummeted to the ground.

"Johnny," he hissed, "you helping me or what?"

He twisted his face to the side, as the light graced his helpless being.

"Get that light off me, Johnny, I want to get home you

know," he screwed his face up tightly as he spoke, not wanting to turn his face back into the pit of thorns.

I let out a small snort of laughter as I observed him squirming in the bush in his comical predicament.

"Come on, there's twigs going up me nose here!"

That only added to my glee, he'd always been the one to get lucky with everything and watch me sort my mess out, now, finally, it was the other way around.

Lobbing my helmet back on top of my throbbing skull I began to shuffle around trying to get out of the aircraft.

I couldn't move.

"Charlie," I hissed in an aggressive whisper, "I can't move, I'm caught in the wire."

The more I stared at my lower legs tangled in the barbed wire, the more the pain grew. The small, rusty spikes had penetrated my clothes and the more I wriggled, the more I felt them pierce my skin. Sweeping the flash-light's gaze away from the bush, I redirected its gaze onto my legs. Small, axe-like daggers had embedded themselves into my shins, and hooked themselves on the under-side of my skin, threatening to rip through the other side and double the size of each fleshy puncture.

Keeping my gloves on I began the excruciating task of picking out the needles one by one, a new bead of blood rolling down my leg with every extraction. The warmth of my blood trickling down my legs felt nice in the midnight chill, almost luxurious. The adrenaline of being in charge of an aircraft gliding to the ground had begun to lose its effect, and my muscles began to cramp up with the cold. The clanging and quiet jingling of the wire as I fiddled with it, rang out across the landscape, as I psyched myself up to pull out the next piece of wire. Every minute twig of wire ripped at my trousers some more, to the point where I possessed nothing more than a piece of fraying fabric, wrapped around my legs. I let my mind wander as I thought about how long it would be before I could get my hands on a new pair. Or if I'd ever make it far enough to need some.

My leather gloves were ruined, great pockmarks of skin beamed out at me, and I could see the sweat glistening in the crevices of my palm. With a grunt of annoyance and frustration, I whipped them off and threw them impatiently to the ground.

"I'm coming, Grandad." How he came to get this nickname bemused me and everyone else he met. He was just a year or two older than me, and by far he was not the oldest on the base. I had been given credit for coming up with this endearing name and yet, I could not pinpoint the moment I had supposedly conjured it up. It was probably one of the many times that I had lost hours of my recollection to the disgusting liquid the Americans classed as Whiskey.

"About time, Boy."

I twisted myself round and gripping the top of the doorway that separated us from the troops, heaved myself feet first through the gap.

They all looked as if they'd been sent into a sleep by a deranged hypnotist. The men sat, legs up on the bench in front of them, heads down into their chest, fast asleep. Their weapons lay ready on their legs, some even with fingers on triggers in anticipation. I could see no faces, just the mesh on top of helmets, a sea of khaki, with no hint of skin, no sign of life.

Only an hour before they had been jovially singing and

bantering with each other, smoking and exchanging stories. Their eyes had told a different story; the upbeat exterior was merely a façade, one that they kept up as each of them fought their own battles as they flew towards death.

Everything was still hauntingly silent. I'd have to come back to them in a minute.

I grabbed my Sten, the cold steel of which was instantly comparable with the midnight air which battered my face, and, as I hopped out, my legs gave way under the excruciating pain, my body landing un-majestically with a solid thump.

The midnight dew began to permeate my skin, refreshing my face and removing from its surface the oily remnants of perspiration. I lay there for a moment, drinking in my surroundings, listening for any sudden changes. I had never experienced silence before. I thought I had, quite often, but lying there I realised what a cacophony of noise I had heard instead of silence. My heart banged like a drum against the inside of my mind, and only in between each pumping motion, did I experience true silence. It was totally barren. My mind wandered as I lay with my eyes closed, and I felt like if I was to reopen them, I should see a totally blank canvas, nothing, just pure, brilliant white. A totally desolate landscape to accompany the neglection of noise.

With a growing agitation, I realised that my previous experience of silence was preferable to the one that I now found myself in. The hatred that I discovered for silence grew as the feeling of an impending doom took a tight grip on me, especially when I was convinced of the barrage of noise that was just moments away.

I had crashed to the ground with such a clatter that I half expected to give away the entire invasion force. I held my breath as I waited for jackboots to squeak across the field and for a hard-nosed German to point a revolver in my general direction.

I found myself hoping that I would never see the bullet exit the revolver, and that I wouldn't know what was going on. I forced my eyelids up, but they wouldn't budge. Maybe the bullet had already come. The silence that I had never before experienced brought with it a peace that I had never encountered before either. This, I thought, was death.

But everything remained perfectly still, a serene silence clinging to the French countryside. The only movement was me. The only noise from my own breathing.

I felt like the only living being among the dead.

I was a ghost.

To download 'All Men are Casualties' head to Amazon now!

'ENEMY HELD TERRITORY' a FREE short story from Thomas Wood is available by going to:
www.ThomasWoodBooks.com/free-book

Printed in Great Britain
by Amazon